Stella Batts
Scaredy Cat

Stella Batts

Scaredy Cat

Book

9

Courtney Sheinmel

Illustrated by Jennifer A. Bell

For Regan S. Hofmann

—Courtney

Sleeping Bear Press™

2395 South Huron Parkway, Suite 200, Ann Arbor, MI 48104
www.sleepingbearpress.com
© Sleeping Bear Press

Ouija® is a registered trademark of Hasbro, Inc., Pop Rocks® is a registered trademark of Zeta Espacial S.A., Raisinets® is a registered trademark of Société des Produits Nestlé S.A., Vevey, Switzerland, Monopoly is a trademark of Hasbro, Inc.

Printed and bound in the United States.
10 9 8 7 6 5 4 3 2 1

Library of Congress Cataloging-in-Publication Data • Names: Sheinmel, Courtney. • Title: Stella Batts : scaredy cat • written by Courtney Sheinmel ; illustrated by Jennifer A. Bell. • Other titles: Scaredy cat • Description: Ann Arbor, MI : Sleeping Bear Press, [2016] | Series: Stella Batts ; book 9 • Summary: "As a prize for reading the most books, Stella's class wins a sleepover in the school library. But after some strange occurrences, including finding a book written by an author who has the same name, Stella realizes she's not as brave as she thought"-Provided by the publisher. • Identifiers: LCCN 2015027636| ISBN 9781585369195 (hard cover) • ISBN 9781585369201 (paperback) • Subjects: | CYAC: Sleepovers–Fiction. | Schools–Fiction. |Fear–Fiction. • Classification: LCC PZ7.S54124 Str 2016 | DDC [Fic]–dc23 • LC record available at http://lccn. loc.gov/2015027636

Table of Contents

CHAPTER 1

Checklist

"Do you have everything you need for school?" Dad asked me on Saturday afternoon.

You're probably wondering why my dad was asking about school on a weekend. Well, I'll tell you: The kids in Mrs. Finkel's third-grade class were having a Somers Elementary School Library Sleepover!

Which meant I was having a library sleepover because *I'm* in Mrs. Finkel's class!

It was the greatest thing that had

happened to me in my whole entire life!

Okay, fine. Maybe not the *greatest* thing . . . getting to meet the star of my favorite TV show was greater. And being a big sister is sometimes greater. And having parents who own a candy store is always really REALLY great.

But a library sleepover was one of the greatest things.

Anyway, back to my conversation with Dad. He was sitting on my bed with my baby brother, Marco, in his lap. Marco likes to be bounced up and down, so that's what Dad was doing. Marco giggled every time. Bounce. Bounce. Bounce. Giggle. Giggle. Giggle.

"Yup, I've got everything I need," I said.

"You like that?" Dad asked Marco. And then he answered for him because Marco is too little to talk for himself. "Yes, you do. Yes, you do."

"Dad, are you listening to me?" I asked.

"What? Oh yes, Stella. I'm sorry."

"Are you sorry you weren't listening to *me*?" Penny asked. Penny is my sister. She's five. She used to be the baby in the family—and sometimes she still wants to be.

"You weren't talking," I reminded her.

"I am now."

"What do you want to tell me?" Dad asked her.

"Um . . ." Penny said.

"You didn't even have anything to say!" I said.

"I have lots of things to say," Penny told me.

"Like what?"

"Like it's not fair that you get to have a sleepover at school!"

"Yes, it is," I said. "You heard what Mr. O'Neil said in assembly on Monday."

Mr. O'Neil is the principal at our school, Somers Elementary School. "I forget," Penny said.

"He said that Mr. Ramos counted up all the books in the library that every class had checked out to read. And Mrs. Finkel's class had checked out more books than anyone else had. So we won the library sleepover, and we get to go to school tonight and bring sleeping bags and have a campout in the library."

(Mr. Ramos is our school librarian, in case you were wondering.)

"It's not fair!" Penny said. "I didn't even know there was a contest! I would have checked out more books!"

"We didn't know there was a contest either," I said. "Mr. O'Neil and Mr. Ramos and all the teachers kept it a secret from all the kids."

It's cool to win a contest you know you entered. But it's even cooler to win a secret contest.

"It's still not fair," Penny said with a pout.

I got my princess hand mirror from the top of my dresser, and went to add it to the top of the pile of things I was bringing to school. "If you keep making that pouty face, it'll freeze that way," I told Penny, which was something my Grandma Dee once said to me.

"No, it won't," Penny said, still pouting. "Let me see."

She grabbed the mirror from me, and I grabbed back. "It's mine," I said, tugging harder. "I'm packing it."

"Girls!" Dad said.

The mirror slipped through both of our

fingers and smashed to the ground. When I picked it back up, there was a crack down the center.

"Oooh," Penny said. "Now you get seven years of bad luck. That's what Bruce from my class says."

I sucked in my breath. "Oh no! But you made me do it."

"Okay, that's enough," Dad said. "It's a

silly superstition. Stella, throw the mirror away and—"

"But it's my favorite."

"It's broken," he said. "You don't need it for the sleepover anyway." He patted the space on the bed next to him. "Penny, come sit here and hold Marco. Stella, where's your list?"

Penny sat down next to Dad and he passed Marco over. He and Penny started to play the tongue game, which is one of the only games Marco can play. And it's not really a game. You just stick your tongue out, and then Marco sticks his tongue out, too.

I gave Dad the piece of paper Mrs. Finkel had passed out on Friday. Across the top it said:

SOMERS ELEMENTARY SCHOOL
SLEEPOVER CHECKLIST

"All right," Dad said. "Let's see what we have here. Number one—sleeping bag?"

"Check!" I said, pointing to the sleeping bag on the floor. "Item number two," Dad said. "Pillow?"

"Check!" I said.

"Hairbrush?"

"Check!"

"Flashlight?"

"Check!"

"Toothbrush and toothpaste?"

"Check and check!"

"What about a change of clothes?" Dad asked.

"That's not on the list."

"But don't you need one?"

"Nope. We get to stay in our pajamas the whole time. Isn't that great?"

"Ow!" Penny cried.

"What happened?" Dad asked.

"Marco pulled my hair," she said. "Bad baby. Bad, bad baby!"

Marco giggled.

"He thinks it's a new game," I told Penny.

"But games are fun and this is not," Penny said. "I don't want to hold him anymore."

"I'll take him back," Dad said.

"Don't pull Daddy's hair, Marco!" Penny said.

"My hair is shorter," Dad told her. "Don't worry."

Dad reached for Marco. And Marco reached for the list! He got the end of it in his little baby fist and he tore a little piece off and tried to eat it.

"No, Marco," I said.

Marco giggled, as if the list tasted like candy. He's never had a treat from Batts

Confections before, so he has no idea what candy should taste like. He has no idea what anything tastes like, besides milk. He doesn't know that paper is gross—grosser than broccoli and brussels sprouts, even. And he doesn't know that fudge is the very best thing to eat in the whole entire world.

"He thinks eating paper is a new game," Penny told me.

"Why don't you change into your pajamas now?" Dad said. "So you'll be ready to go when Mom comes home."

"I am wearing my pajamas," I told him.

"Those are your regular leggings," Penny said. "And a regular pink shirt."

"Well, Evie and I want to wear matching pajamas, but we don't have any that match. But we do each have leggings and T-shirts."

"I'm going to sleep in my purple leggings

and a pink T-shirt tonight, too," Penny said.

"But Penny," I said. "You can wear your real pajamas. You don't have to be the same."

"I want to be," she said.

"Dad, she's copying me," I said.

Penny stuck her tongue out.

"And now she's sticking her tongue out," I added.

"It's the tongue game," she said. "You're supposed to copy me."

"That's only for babies," I told her.

"Goo goo ga ga," Penny said. "I'm copying Marco now."

"You know what's good about being a big kindergarten girl?" Dad asked.

"What?" Penny asked.

"You are learning to read. Why don't you read the last item on Stella's list?"

She looked over my shoulder and started

to sound it out. "Li . . . li . . . Libbb."

"Library card," I finished for her. "Check! That's it! That's the end of the list!"

"Stella!" Penny cried. "That was my word to read!"

"I was just helping you," I said.

"Dad, tell her it was supposed to be my word," Penny said.

"Girls," Dad started. But then he stopped himself.

"What?" I asked.

"Do you hear that?"

Penny and I listened closely. We heard the sound of the front door opening and closing. And then we heard Mom's voice calling, "Anyone home?"

"Mom's home!" Penny shouted.

"Thank goodness," I heard Dad say, softly to himself.

Penny took off down the hall to see Mom. Dad followed her, with Marco in his arms. I picked up my backpack with all my stuff in it, plus my sleeping bag and pillow, and walked down the hall to the rest of my family.

"I'm ready to go," I announced. I bent down to put on my shoes.

"It's still not fair," Penny said.

"Sure it is," I said. "Our class won fair and square."

"But I've always wanted to see what school looks like on the weekend."

"It looks the same as it does on weekdays," Mom told her.

"Besides," Dad said. "If you went to school tonight, you wouldn't get to work on the Super-Secret Dad-and-Penny Project I have planned."

"A secret plan like a secret contest?" she asked.

"You got it," Dad said.

"So what is it?"

"It's super-secret," Dad told her. "But I'll tell you if you stay home with me."

"Okay!" Penny said.

I gave everyone hugs good-bye, except for Mom because she was going to drive me to school. When I hugged Dad I whispered to him, "Is there really a secret project, or did you just make it up to distract Penny?"

"It's a secret," he whispered back.

I was pretty sure that meant he'd just made it up. I wondered what would happen when Penny found out there wasn't really a secret. But I didn't get to find out because it was time to go.

Mom helped me carry the stuff to the car. I buckled my seat belt, and we were off!

CHAPTER 2

Check In

Mom and I went straight to the library. A bunch of kids from my class were already there in the big front room. Mostly the boys. They were all wearing pajamas, and unrolling their sleeping bags on the floor.

The librarian, Mr. Ramos, was at his desk. He was wearing blue-and-green plaid pajamas—a button-down top and pants. I'd never seen a teacher (or a librarian) in pajamas before!

"Hey there, Batts ladies," Mrs. Anderson said, walking toward us. She's my friend Lucy's mom. She was also in pajamas. Hers were purple fleece. My mom was wearing regular clothes—brown corduroy pants and a blue shirt.

"Were parents supposed to wear pajamas to drop us off?" I asked.

"Only the parent chaperones," Mrs. Anderson said. "That's me and Asher's dad." She pointed across the room. I saw Mr. Haskell—Asher's dad—in the computer area.

"I didn't know parents could stay over too," I said.

"Sorry, Stel," Mom said. "I chaperoned the last field trip."

The last field trip was to our candy store, Batts Confections.

"A field trip means a trip outside of

school," I said. "This isn't a field trip because we're staying in school. But that's okay. It's my first sleepover and it wouldn't really count if you were here."

"Of course," Mom said. She gave Mrs. Anderson a wink.

"I saw that!" I told her.

Suddenly there was a crash across the room. We all turned to see Joshua standing next to a pile of board games that had fallen off a shelf and onto the floor. "It wasn't my fault," he said quickly.

Mom and Mrs. Anderson went over to help him, and I followed. I've never actually played any of the library board games before, but maybe they were for special occasions. Like sleepovers.

Joshua picked up the Monopoly money and stuffed it into the box. "Let's try and do this neatly," Mrs. Anderson said.

Mom bent to pick up another fallen game. "Oh, a Ouija board," she said. "I haven't seen one of these in years."

The word on the box said: OUIJA. But Mom was pronouncing it like: WEE-GEE.

"Is it a good game?" I asked.

"It's not exactly a game," she said. "My friend Dawn and I used to play." She scrunched

up her face like she was deciding whether to tell me something.

"What?" I asked.

"Well, the point of it is to talk to ghosts," she said.

"Ghosts?!"

"It was just a game," she told me.

"I thought you said it wasn't a game."

"It's make-believe," she said. "Ghosts aren't real."

"I still don't want to play it," I said.

"Don't worry," Mrs. Anderson said. "The Ouija board is not on the schedule tonight. None of the board games are. We have a lot of other fun things planned. Why don't you set up your stuff with your friends? The girls are all in the back half of the library. Mrs. Finkel and I will be sleeping back there with you. Mr. Haskell and Mr. Ramos will stay in front with the boys."

"Okay," I said.

I hugged Mom good-bye, and then I skipped to the back of the library. Well, I skipped as well as I could while also carrying all my stuff.

"Hey!" I called to my friends—Lucy, along with Arielle, and Talisa. They'd set up in the Young Readers reading corner. That meant the books that had pictures in them. Those books used to be on the shelf by Mr. Ramos's desk, but now they had a whole corner. It was Penny's favorite spot in the library. I felt a little bit bad that she didn't get to be here, since I'd be sleeping in her favorite spot.

"Oh good, you're here," Lucy said.

Everyone had unrolled their sleeping bags onto the floor. But there was space for two more sleeping bags—one next to Lucy, and one next to Arielle.

I put my sleeping bag down. "Can you guys move over a little so Evie can sleep next to me? We're wearing the same pajamas tonight."

Lucy looked me up and down. "You're not even wearing pajamas," she said. "I saw you wear that shirt to school last week—it's a regular shirt. And those are regular leggings."

"Evie and I didn't have real pajamas that matched," I explained. "But these are comfy enough to sleep in."

"I like them," Arielle said, softly of course. Arielle always talks softly. And Lucy is always a bit loud. I wished she would be more quiet about my not wearing real pajamas.

Everyone squished over so there was room next to me for Evie's sleeping bag. Then Mrs. Finkel came over to tell us we had three minutes before we had to meet the group at the big table to learn about the first activity of the night.

"What's that?" Talisa asked.

"You'll have to come out to the big table to find out," Mrs. Finkel said.

In case you were wondering, Mrs. Finkel was wearing pajamas too. Sort of. She had on gray pants that looked like they could be pajamas, or they could just be regular pants. On top she had a gray sweatshirt that said COLUMBIA on it.

"What's Columbia?" I asked.

"It's a college," she said.

"Is it where you went to college?" Lucy asked.

"No, my husband did," she said.

Usually your teachers are just your teachers and you don't get to know anything about their outside lives. But now I knew a few things about Mrs. Finkel when she wasn't at school:

1. She has a son named Evan

2. She has a dog named Shadow

3. She has a husband who went to college at Columbia

"What's your husband's name?" I asked.

"Mr. Finkel," she said. "Now there are just two minutes left, girls."

She left us to go tell the other kids about our meeting at the big table. Lucy, Arielle, Talisa, and I walked over. There weren't four seats left together so we sat two and two. Lucy and Arielle sat on the side of the table with Clark and Asher. Talisa and I sat on the other side of the table . . . with Joshua.

In case you haven't read my other books or you forgot, I'll remind you: Joshua is the biggest meanie in our class. Except sometimes

he's not a meanie. Sometimes he's even my friend. I never know which way he's going to be—a meanie or my friend. It's very confusing.

The only empty seat was right next to him so I took it.

"Hello, kids," Mr. Ramos said.

"Hello, Mr. Ramos," we said back.

"First I want to congratulate you on being such good readers."

Mrs. Finkel, Mrs. Anderson, and Mr. Haskell started clapping for us, so us kids clapped, too.

When the clapping stopped, Mr. Ramos went on. "Reading is its own reward," he said. "But this sleepover is a bonus. We've planned a very fun night. There are just a few rules we need to go over before we get started."

"Ugh, rules!" Joshua said. "We shouldn't have rules on weekends!"

"One of the rules is being quiet when Mr. Ramos is talking to the group," Mrs. Finkel said. Mrs. Finkel has a lot of rules for weekdays, in our class. She calls them Ground Rules. If you break them, you get sent to the principal's office.

Mr. Ramos told us the rules for the sleepover, which were things like, "No bringing food back into the library," and "Lights out at nine o'clock."

"That means all twenty of your flashlights, too," Mrs. Finkel added. "Flashlights are for emergencies only."

"Any questions?" Mr. Ramos asked.

I raised my hand. "Yes, Stella?"

"Didn't Mrs. Finkel mean *twenty-two* flashlights?" I asked. "There are twenty-two kids in our class, so we have twenty-two flashlights."

"I meant twenty," Mrs. Finkel said. "Maddie is away with her family, and Evie wasn't able to come at the last minute."

"But Evie is coming," I said. "She's just a little bit late."

"No," Mr. Haskell said. He glanced at Mrs. Finkel, and she gave a slight head shake. "I spoke to her mother a little while ago. She's a bit under the weather."

Lucy looked over at me and my non-pajama pajamas. "That's bad luck that you're wearing that outfit and she's not even here," she whispered.

"Yeah," I whispered back.

"Any more questions?" Mr. Ramos asked.

There weren't any, so Mrs. Finkel asked for a volunteer to hand some papers and pencils out for our first activity. Lots of kids raised their hands, but I didn't. I was too busy wondering about Evie. Why hadn't she called *me* to say she wasn't coming?

Joshua called out, "Pick me! Mrs. Finkel, pick me!" But Mrs. Finkel never picks on kids who call out. She picked Talisa and a boy named Cooper instead.

Joshua leaned over and whispered in my ear. "Hey, Smella, want to know a secret?" he said.

"Sure," I told him.

"Ghosts are too real," he said. "And I can prove it."

CHAPTER 3

Scavenger Hunt

Talisa gave me a piece of paper. Across the top were these words:

SOMERS ELEMENTARY SCHOOL
LIBRARY SCAVENGER HUNT

"Just a few rules before we get started," Mr. Ramos said.

"Ugh, more rules," Joshua said.

"Every game has rules, and this one is no

exception," Mr. Ramos went on. "There will be four people to a team. We have twenty kids, as Mrs. Finkel said, so that's five perfectly equal teams of four. You should stay with your team the whole time. When you find something on the list, write it down in the space on your sheet, and then leave the item where you found it so other people can have a chance."

"But if we move it, we have a better chance at winning," Lucy said.

"That sounds like cheating," Mrs. Anderson said sternly.

Lucy sat back in her chair and folded her arms across her chest. "I was just saying," she said.

"There is no cheating," Mrs. Finkel said. "Be respectful of people who are not on your team. A cheating team is a losing team."

"That's right," Mr. Ramos said. "And the

final rule is stay inside the library. Everything you need is here. Any questions?"

Joshua called out, "Can we play the Ouija board instead?"

"No," Mrs. Finkel told him. "And no calling out. Let's try being respectful of each other, okay, Joshua?"

No Calling Out is one of our weekday classroom Ground Rules. Joshua folded his arms across his chest. Another kid named Clark raised his hand and Mr. Ramos called on him. "Is there a prize?" he asked.

"Yes, there is," Mr. Ramos said. And before anyone could ask what it was, he added, "And you will find out what it is when we declare the winner."

"Aw, man," Joshua said. "I wanted to know right now."

Sometimes Joshua says things that the

rest of us are thinking. But Mrs. Finkel gave him a look that said: *Don't call out again, or I'll send you to the principal.* I wondered if Mr. O'Neil was here on the weekend, too.

"Now you'll have a few minutes to confer with your group before we get started," Mr. Ramos said.

Talisa, Arielle, and Lucy bent their heads together. "Wait, I have a question," I said.

"Yes, Stella?"

"What does that word mean that you just said?"

"What word?"

"Um," I said. It's hard to remember a word when you don't know what it means. But I love learning new words. The more words I know, the more words I can put in my books. "Con, something."

"Confer?"

"Yeah, that one."

"It means to talk to each other and figure out your strategy."

"Okay?" Mrs. Finkel asked.

I shook my head. "Now I have another question. What does strategy mean?"

"It means your plan."

Of course I knew what plan meant, so I was all set. "Thanks," I said.

I bent my head toward the other girls' so we could confer quietly. "This is what I think," Lucy said, her voice just a whisper. "We should each have jobs. Arielle's job will be holding the list. Talisa's job will be deciding what order to find things. Stella's job will be writing things down."

"What's your job?" Talisa asked.

"I'll tell us where to go," she said.

Lucy can be a little bossy sometimes,

but it was okay because I wanted the writing-down job anyway.

"All right, is everyone ready?" Mrs. Anderson asked.

All us kids chorused, "Yes!"

"On your marks, get set, go!"

"Okay," Talisa told us. "I've decided we're going to start with the first thing. A book under a hundred pages."

"I know where the kindergarten books are," I said. "They're right—"

"Wait," Lucy cut me off. "It's my job to tell you where to go. And anyway, I remember from when we were in kindergarten. They're right next to Mr. Ramos's desk."

"No, they moved them to the back," I said. "Right where we're sleeping. We should go there."

"Okay, fine," Lucy said. "But when we get

there, I'll write it down this time so it's fair."

We raced to the Young Readers corner. When we got there, we didn't know who was supposed to pull the book off the shelf. I grabbed one that Penny had read last month—*Days With Frog and Toad* by Arnold Lobel—and I flipped to the last page. "It's sixty-four pages," I said.

EXPLORE WITH BOOKS!

"*I'll* write it down," Lucy said.

She took the pencil that Cooper had given to me, and wrote *Days With Frog and Toad* on the blank line.

Talisa looked back at the list. "Now we have to find a book that's OVER two hundred pages."

"Let's go to the fantasy section," Lucy said. "My sister says they are the longest books."

This time Lucy took a book off the shelf. She picked the one that had the biggest binding, and when she flipped to the back we couldn't believe how many pages it was—six hundred and fifty-two pages! I'd have to write at least five books to have that many!

I wrote the name of the book down, and then Talisa told us the next item on the list. "Find a book with purple writing on the cover."

That was harder to find, because none of us could remember a book with purple writing on the cover, so we kept having to pull books off the shelf (and put them back) until we found one. But finally we did. I wrote it down, and we moved on to the next thing—a book with a unicorn on the cover. And the next thing—a book with a flower. And the one after that. And the one after that.

"What's next?" I asked, after we'd found a book dedicated to someone with the same first name as someone in our class.

"Now we have to find a book that was published at least ten years ago," Talisa said. "But how do we know when it was published?"

"Maybe if it looks really old we'll know it's at least ten," Lucy said.

"But sometimes books look old even after just a little bit of time," Arielle said softly.

"Like if you bend the binding, or doggy-ear the pages."

I never do that with my books. But it didn't matter, because I knew how to check how old a book was. "You can tell what year a book was published because it says it, right inside," I told them. I took a book off the shelf, and flipped a couple pages. "Look. This one was published two years ago."

"Okay, we need an older one," Talisa said.

"Obviously," Lucy said. "Let's go over there." She pointed to the biographies section. "Biographies are usually written about old people. Maybe we'll find an old book."

"That's a great idea," Arielle said.

Lucy took a book off the shelf and flipped to the page with the date. "Eight years old," she said. Which is the same age all of us are. "Too young."

Talisa picked out a book, but it was only four years old. Then Arielle picked a book, but it was only seven years old.

Then I picked one. It was called *My Missing Friend*. "Hey look, this is weird," I said. "The author's name is Stella B."

My friends all looked. "This is your book?" Talisa asked.

I shook my head. "None of my books are in the library—at least not yet," I said. I flipped to the date page. "Besides, this one was written in nineteen thirty-three."

"That's definitely more than ten years old!" Lucy said. "Write it down!"

Arielle held up the clipboard and I wrote down the name of the book.

"What's next?"

"Oooooh eeeeeee," someone said. It was so soft, almost a whisper.

"What did you say?" I asked.

"I didn't say anything," Lucy said.

"Someone did," I said.

"I didn't hear anything," Talisa said.

"Me either," Arielle said.

"Ooooooh eeeeeee oooooooooooooooh!" came the voice again. Still whispery, but a little bit louder this time.

"I heard that," Arielle said in a shaky voice.

"Me too," Talisa said.

I started to get a prickly feeling all over.

"Who's there?" Lucy demanded.

"It's the library ghost," the voice said. But this time instead of sounding whispery it sounded familiar.

"JOSHUA!" my friends and I cried out at the same time.

He came around from behind the biography shelf. "What are you guys doing?"

"None of your beeswax," Lucy told him.

I slipped the old book back on the shelf and stood in front of it so he couldn't see. "Why aren't you with your group?" I asked.

"That's none of *your* beeswax," he said.

"Hey, kids," Mrs. Anderson said. "How's it going?"

"Fine," Joshua said quickly.

"Actually," Lucy said to her mom. "Joshua isn't supposed to be in our group."

"I lost my group," Joshua said.

Mrs. Anderson held out a hand toward him. "Why don't we go find them?" she said, and she led him away.

"Whew," Lucy said. "Good thing my mom's here."

"Did you want your mom to chaperone?" I asked her.

" 'Course I did. Why?"

I shrugged. "I didn't want my mom to stay tonight—then it would feel too much like sleeping at home."

"She's not sleeping next to us," Lucy said. "We might not even be able to see her."

"You guys," Talisa said. "We have one more thing to find."

"What?" Arielle asked.

"We each have to pick a book to read tonight, and bring it to Mr. Ramos's desk for checkout."

I knew exactly what book I was going to read. The book by the other Stella B. I pulled it off the shelf. The other girls raced around looking for their own books. Since we had to stick together, we raced together.

"No running!" Mrs. Finkel called.

How did she expect us to win if we weren't allowed to run?

When Talisa, Lucy, and Arielle had their books, we went to Mr. Ramos's desk. He was talking to someone on his cell phone.

"Excuse me, are we first?" Lucy asked, but Mr. Ramos held up two fingers and mouthed the words "two seconds."

I happen to know when a grown-up says it'll be two seconds they mean much longer.

I turned my book over to read what it was about. Because we'd been rushing, I didn't get to see.

Stella B and her best friend did everything together: They read all the same books, and sang all the same songs. They even cut clothes from the same cloth and made matching outfits.

But one day Stella's best friend didn't show up when she was supposed to.

A chill went up my spine and I shuddered. "What's wrong?" Talisa asked.

"In the book the other Stella B's friend went missing," I said. "She was supposed to show up, and she didn't. Just like . . ."

"Just like Evie," Arielle quietly supplied.

I felt another chill, and shuddered again as I nodded.

"Oh, come on, you guys," Lucy said. "You heard what Asher's dad said. He said Evie is under the weather. That means sick."

"But did you see the looks he and Mrs. Finkel gave each other when he said it?" I asked.

Lucy rolled her eyes.

"I wasn't looking at him so I didn't see,"

Arielle admitted.

"I was," Talisa said. "I saw. She shook her head."

"That's right, she did," I said. I put *My Missing Friend* down on the desk. "I don't want to read this. I'm going to get another book."

I went right to the chapter book section. "Where's your group, Stella?" Mrs. Finkel asked.

"Over there," I said quickly. I was talking fast because I didn't have much time.

"You're supposed to be all together."

I grabbed a book off the shelf—I'd read it before, so I knew it wasn't too scary. "I just had to get this," I said, and I raced back over to my friends.

"Where's Mr. Ramos?" I asked.

"He went out into the hall," Arielle said.

"So now what?" I asked.

"Mo-om!" Lucy called. "We're all done and Mr. Ramos isn't here. Now what?"

Mrs. Anderson told us to write our names on sticky notes and stick them on our books so Mr. Ramos could check them out when he came back. The next group finished, and the next. Everyone put sticky notes on their books. We left them in a pile on Mr. Ramos's desk, and we handed our sheets up to Mrs. Finkel.

"Did we win?" Lucy asked.

"We'll check your answers while you're at dinner, and announce the winner when you return, but right now it's time for dinner."

CHAPTER 4

Pizza Party!

The lunchroom was WAY different at night. First of all, there were only four tables set up. The rest of the tables were folded up and pushed against the walls. Second of all, most of the lights were out, except for the ones above the four tables. The rest of the room looked dark, and kind of spooky. And third of all, one of the tables had a bunch of pizza boxes on top of it.

The pizza was the good news. The bad

news was Mr. Moyers was in the lunchroom, too.

"Bad luck again," Lucy told me.

"What did you say?" I asked.

"I said bad luck," she told me.

"I'll say," Talisa said.

Arielle didn't say anything. She just stood beside us, looking shaky.

I thought about what Penny had said happened when you broke a mirror—seven years of bad luck. Dad had said it wasn't true, and I wanted to believe him. But first Evie didn't show up, and now this.

Mr. Moyers is the mean lunch aide. You can tell how mean he is just by looking at him. He's got beady little Raisinet eyes, and a long pointy nose, and thin lips that are pressed together like he's just tasted something sour. When he does open his mouth, it is never to talk in a regular voice. I don't know if Mr. Moyers even *has* a regular voice. I've only ever heard him yelling. And he yells about EVERYTHING. If you spill something by accident. If you want to trade desserts. Or if more than two kids have to go to the bathroom at the same time.

Mr. Moyers turned and fixed his beady little eyes on me and my friends. "Don't stand around like deer in headlights!" he yelled. "Sit down!"

We raced around and sat at the table that was farthest away from him. There were paper plates and juice boxes set up at every seat. I could smell the pizza from my seat and it was making me feel EXTRA STARVING. Pizza is my number one favorite food in the whole entire world. Well, except for fudge. If I was only allowed to eat one thing for the rest of my life it would be fudge. But if I got to eat two things, I'd pick fudge *and* pizza.

Other kids who hadn't been yelled at had walked over to the pizza table. They reached for the open boxes, and said things like, "Wait, I don't want a plain slice!" And, "Hey is that the pepperoni?"

But soon Mr. Moyers yelled at them, too. "Don't touch other people's food with your dirty little hands!"

Clark was so startled he dropped a piece of pizza facedown on the floor.

"Now look what you did!" Mr. Moyers shouted. He sure does know how to make pizza parties stop being fun.

Mrs. Anderson stuck two fingers in her mouth and whistled the loudest whistle I'd ever heard. Everyone got quiet. Mr. Moyers narrowed his beady eyes into little slits, but he

got quiet, too.

"Everyone, please take your seats," Mrs. Anderson said.

"But I didn't get any pizza yet!" Joshua said.

"Sit, Joshua," Mrs. Finkel told him. "Whether you have pizza or not."

"Aw, man!" Joshua said. But he sat down—at the very same table my friends and I were sitting at.

"Now—" Mrs. Finkel started.

"NOW!" Mr. Moyers shouted. "All of you kids have not behaved well since you walked in that door!"

But that wasn't true! No one was being bad, and some of us were being really, REALLY good. Like Arielle. She had her hands folded on the table like she was sitting at her desk in Mrs. Finkel's classroom. But did Mr. Moyers say anything about that? No, he did not. Because he's too mean to notice the nice things.

"Hang on," Mrs. Anderson told him. "The kids have been behaving just fine. We didn't give them instructions before we walked in here. And that's our fault—not theirs."

Talisa, Arielle, Joshua, and I looked at Lucy with our eyes open wide. We couldn't believe what her mom did. First of all, you don't usually hear a grown-up admitting they did a wrong thing. And second, I'd never ever seen anyone stand up to Mr. Moyers before!

Mr. Moyers's eyes were scrunched up even smaller, and his lips were pressed together so tight you almost couldn't see them anymore. When he turned he saw me looking at him, and my cheeks turned hot like I was eating spicy candy. I looked away as quickly as possible, pretending it had never happened in the first place.

"Please raise your hand if you do not have a slice yet," Mrs. Anderson said.

Most kids raised their hands. Mrs. Anderson, Mrs. Finkel, and Mr. Haskell went around bringing pizza to everyone. We had a choice between plain, pepperoni, or veggie. I picked plain.

Mr. Moyers stood off to the side,

grumbling about coming in to school on a weekend to be with ungrateful kids. But he was wrong about us. We were super grateful about winning the secret contest and getting pizza. The only thing we were ungrateful about was him.

I finished my slice pretty quickly since it was so delicious. I sneaked one more look over at Mr. Moyers, but he wasn't there anymore.

"I wonder where Mr. Moyers went," I said.

"Maybe he left because he hates us so much," Lucy said.

"I wonder why he works here if he hates kids," Arielle said.

"Knock knock," Talisa said.

"Who's there?" Lucy, Arielle, and I asked at the same time.

"The ghost!" Joshua answered.

"You're not supposed to answer," Lucy told him. "You're not supposed to be playing at all."

"Ooooooh eeeeeee," Joshua said. "I'm a ghost."

"Stop it," I told him. "Ghosts aren't real."

"You can't know that for sure," Joshua said.

"I've never seen any," I told him.

"Plenty of things are real that you can't see," Joshua said. "Like the wind, or the sound of things, or having feelings."

"Those things are different," I said.

"How?" Joshua asked.

"They just are," I said.

"That's not a good answer."

In my head, I knew it wasn't. I just wanted it to be.

"Joshua," Lucy said. "You should go to another table. You are not our friend."

"I'm Stella's friend," he said.

But I shook my head. He didn't feel like my friend just then.

"Go on," Lucy said. "Or I'll tell my mom."

"See if I care if you tell her," Joshua said. But he stood up to leave. He picked up his plate, which had his crust left over, and his juice box. Then he took a couple steps closer to me. My stomach started jumping like Pop Rocks. I was afraid he was going to say something about thinking we were friends. I didn't know how to explain that sometimes we were friends and sometimes we weren't.

But I didn't have to, because right then was when Mr. Moyers reappeared. "Sit back down, young man!" he thundered.

Everything seemed to happen in slow motion after that, but there was nothing I could do to stop it. Joshua startled and fell backward. His plate and juice box went flying. Usually juice boxes only have eensy weensy holes on top where you put the straw in. But Joshua had opened his up all the way on top. All the juice spilled out—onto me!

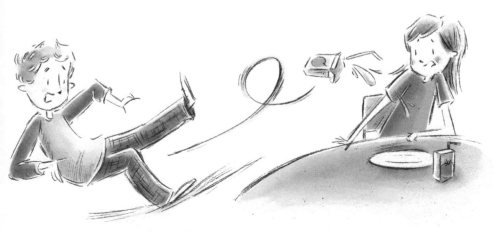

CHAPTER 5

It's Only a Story

I dried my shirt as best I could with the hand dryer in the bathroom, but it was still a bit damp. Then it was time to go back to the library. Mrs. Finkel told us to sit around the big table.

"Did everyone have a nice dinner?" Mr. Ramos asked. He hadn't eaten yet, since he'd stayed behind in the library to look over our scavenger hunt answers. Mrs. Finkel had brought back three slices of pizza—one of each kind—and they were sitting on his desk waiting to be gobbled up.

"Yes," we chorused.

"That's good to hear," he said. "And now the moment we've all been waiting for. Drum-roll, please." A few of the boys beat their hands against the top of the table. "And the winners are . . . Lucy Anderson, Stella Batts, Talisa Lee, and Arielle Waldorf!"

Lucy, Talisa, Arielle, and I looked at each other and grinned. The other kids clapped for us. Except Joshua. He shouted out, "Boo!" We all ignored him.

"We get a prize, right?" Talisa asked.

"You sure do," Mr. Ramos said. He went behind his desk and came back with . . . socks. Four pairs, each striped blue and gold. "Those are the school colors," he explained.

Up till then I didn't even know we had

school colors.

"They're so cozy," Arielle said. She brought them up to her cheek.

"Ew! Your face will smell like feet!" Joshua said.

"She hasn't even worn them yet," Lucy said. "You're just jealous."

"That's enough, Lucy," Mrs. Anderson said.

But I could tell she sort of agreed with her.

I kicked my shoes off under the table and started to put my new socks on. But Mrs. Finkel said, "No, Stella. Keep your shoes on until it's time for bed. We don't want anyone slipping and falling."

I don't know how Mrs. Finkel thought

I could possibly slip and fall while we were sitting at the table! But I left my socks in my lap and Mr. Ramos announced the next activity, which was a group story. He would say the first sentence, and then we'd go around the table and each say a sentence—in the end it would be twenty-four sentences (twenty kids plus four grown-ups) and that would equal a whole story.

"No!" Joshua called out.

"Joshua!" Mrs. Finkel said.

Joshua raised his hand, and then she called on him. "I wanted to do the Ouija board," he said. "It's a sleepover. We should do spooky things, like talk to ghosts."

"Yeah!" a bunch of other kids agreed.

"Well, Mr. Ramos planned another activity," Mrs. Finkel said.

"Hang on," Mr. Ramos said. "I'm not

married to the idea of a group story. We can put it to a vote."

Then *I* raised my hand. "Yes, Stella?" Mrs. Finkel said.

"You can't be married to an idea," I said. "You have to be married to a person."

"Actually," Mr. Ramos said. "You can use the word 'married' to reference other things that are connected or joined. It's not as common to use the word that way, but it's still correct."

"Cool," I said. I love learning new words, and that includes learning that words I already knew could mean different things.

I started thinking about ideas *I* was married to, like: I was married to the idea that fudge is the very best treat. And I was married to the idea that—

"Okay, it looks like the Ouija board voters win!" Mrs. Anderson declared.

Oh no! I'd been so busy thinking about ideas I was married to that I didn't get to vote. More bad luck!

Mr. Haskell got the game down from the shelf, and put the board on the table. It was a big, flat wooden board with the letters A through Z and numbers 0 through 9 written on it, plus the words "yes," "no," and "good-bye." We were supposed to put our hands on a moveable piece, shaped kind of like a triangle. Then we'd ask questions, and whatever ghosts or spirits were around would guide the triangle around the board to spell out the answers. But since there were so many of us—twenty kids, plus four adults—and the triangle was pretty small, Mrs. Anderson suggested that only a couple kids put their hands on it, and the rest of us would hold hands around the table. Joshua and Lucy got to be the ones to touch the piece, which was fine with me. I didn't want to do it. Arielle held my left hand and Talisa held my right one.

"So who gets to say the first question?" Asher asked. "And what should it be?"

"I'll ask the first question since it was my idea," Joshua said. "And my question is: Are there any ghosts in here?"

The triangle seemed to shake a little bit

beneath their fingers. Then it slid to yes.

"Ooooh," Clark said.

"You made it move that way," Lucy said.

"No, I didn't," Joshua said. "There really is a ghost. Ask it something."

"Do you have a message for anyone?" Lucy asked.

Their hands were on the triangle, and it began to move. First to an S. Then an M. Then an E. Then L.

S-M-E-L. Two more letters and you'd have my name. Or not my real name, but you'd have "Smella," which is what Joshua always calls me. Maybe the ghost called me that, too. My heart was POUNDING!

"Joshua! You are moving it again!" Lucy cried.

"I am not!"

"Someone else should hold it."

"I will! I will!" kids called out.

"No!" Joshua said.

"Everyone should get a turn, Joshua," Mrs. Finkel told him. She picked a girl named Ruby to take his place. Ruby and Joshua switched seats, and Ruby put a hand on the Ouija triangle. I couldn't look anymore, so I looked to the side. Next to me, Arielle was squeezing her eyes shut. Her palm was sweaty in mine. And just behind her—

"EEEEEEEEE!!!!!!!!!!!!!!!!!!!" I screamed.

"Stella, what happened?" Mrs. Finkel said.

"I saw yellow eyes!"

"Where?"

"Over there!" I pointed to one of the shelves. It looked normal now, but just seconds before, there had been a pair of yellow eyes staring at me from between books.

"Nothing's there," Mrs. Finkel said.

"Sometimes our eyes play tricks on us," Mrs. Anderson added.

"They weren't playing tricks," I insisted. "I know what I saw."

"It's the ghost!" Arielle cried out. It was the first time I'd ever heard Arielle say anything loudly.

"Told you there was a ghost in here," Joshua said. "They always disappear when people are trying to look for them."

"Oooooh," Talisa said.

"You know what," Mr. Ramos said. "I think I'm married to the idea of a group story after all. Let's pack this up and start the activity over."

"No!" Joshua said.

But Mr. Ramos was already describing how the group story game worked. We'd stay in a circle around the table, and he'd say a sentence that was the beginning of the story. Then the next person would go, and then the next, and that's how we'd craft a story all together. "So here we go," Mr. Ramos said. "Once upon a time there were twenty boys and girls, and four adults, and they were having a sleepover in the library, when something unexpected happened."

"The unexpected thing was a visitor," said Miles, the boy sitting on the right next to him.

"Now Eleanor," Mr. Ramos said, nodding to the girl next to Miles.

"She had a message to give to all the kids," Eleanor said.

"And now Beatrice," said Mr. Ramos.

"The message was a little bit . . . um . . . it was from a ghost."

It was Clark's turn. He said, "Someone is going to have really bad luck tonight."

Then it was Mrs. Finkel's turn. "But she said if everyone had good behavior, there would be a lot of good luck."

After that kids continued to go around, adding to the story, but I couldn't concentrate on what they were saying. All I could think about were the ghosty yellow eyes, and bad luck, and maybe that was the message it had to give to me. Maybe Penny was right about the mirror, and I was in for seven years of bad luck.

I was only eight years old. Seven years was practically my whole life!

"SMELLA!" Joshua called out.

"What?" I asked.

Everyone laughed. Even the four grown-ups were smiling. "It's your turn, dear," Mrs. Anderson said.

"Oh, I . . . I didn't hear what just happened."

"She wasn't listening!" Joshua said in a singsongy voice. "She has to go to the principal!"

"Mr. O'Neil isn't here," Mrs. Finkel said. "But if you keep up this behavior, you'll have to go home."

"I wasn't the one not listening," Joshua said.

"We can skip you for now," Mr. Ramos said.

"Okay," I said.

I listened for the rest of the story. In the story a ghost had come to the library, but everyone had convinced it to leave. Joshua was the last kid. He said, "Then the ghost said Smella—"

"Joshua," Mrs. Finkel warned.

"Fine. Then the ghost said that Stella had to go back to the ghost world with him. The end!"

"That's not the end!" Lucy said. "Stella didn't even get to go yet."

"She wasn't listening," Joshua said. "That means she skipped her turn."

"Does not."

"Does so."

"Stella, do you have anything to add?" Mr. Ramos asked.

I shook my head.

"That's all right," Mrs. Finkel said. "Stella knows it's only a game. Everything we played tonight was only a game."

"Do we get to play another one now?"

Talisa asked.

"Now it's time to go to the bathroom, brush your teeth, and wash your faces. When you're done, you may go back to your sleeping bags and the books you picked out will be waiting for you."

I guess I still looked scared, because Mrs. Anderson said, "All right, Stella?"

"Yeah, all right," I said.

I was happy to leave the table, and group games, and especially Joshua.

Speaking of Joshua, Mrs. Finkel said she wanted to speak to him privately in the hall for a few minutes. "Aw, man!" Joshua said.

My friends and I headed back to our sleeping bags to grab our toothbrushes. We were holding our cozy socks in our hands. But I dropped mine when I saw what was lying on top of my sleeping bag!

CHAPTER 6

The Wrong Book

It was *My Missing Friend* by Stella B—the other Stella B.

"Oh no!" I said. "It's the wrong book—the scary book!"

"Oooh, Stella," Arielle said in her softly-soft voice. "You don't think it's because . . . well, because . . ."

"Because what?" I asked.

"Because of what Joshua said about bad luck?"

"Oh no," Lucy broke in. "Mr. Ramos put our books down way before Joshua said that. And besides, he was just making things up to be mean."

"But I broke a mirror at home before I came here. And that's SEVEN YEARS of bad luck. Penny said."

"Oooh," Arielle said again.

"Penny's only in kindergarten," Lucy told me.

"But lots of bad luck things have happened," I reminded her.

"Seeing a ghost doesn't count as bad luck."

"It doesn't count as good luck," I said.

"And other things happened, too. Like getting spilled on, and now getting the wrong book."

"Just bring the book back to Mr. Ramos," Talisa said. "He'll let you trade it in for the book you wanted."

So that's what I did. I picked the book up by its corner, and I held it as far out in front of me as I could, as if it smelled bad.

Mr. Ramos was sitting at his desk eating his pizza, even though it was pretty late for dinner, and he had told us we weren't allowed to eat in the library. Sometimes

grown-ups don't obey the rules that they make for kids.

"Excuse me, Mr. Ramos," I said.

Mr. Ramos chewed and swallowed. "Yes, Stella?"

I put *My Missing Friend* down on the desk. "This wasn't the book I was supposed to get," I said. "I wanted *Tales of a Fourth Grade Nothing*."

"I know," Mr. Ramos said. "I made a switch."

"But I thought we were allowed to pick our own books."

"You are—but when I was checking *Tales of a Fourth Grade Nothing* out for you, I realized you'd read it before."

"It was one of my favorites," I said.

"I'm happy to hear that," he said. "But I thought maybe you'd want to try something new tonight. This book—*My Missing Friend*—looked pretty interesting to me. And look at the name of the author!"

It was at that exact moment that Mrs. Finkel and Joshua came back in the library. "Who's the author?" Joshua asked. He leaned over to look at the book. "Stella B? No way! You can't write books. You're only eight."

"I can *too* write books," I told him. "But I didn't write this one. A different Stella B did—in nineteen thirty-three. She might not . . . well, she's probably not even alive anymore."

"Maybe she was the ghost trying to talk to you," Joshua said. "Or maybe . . . maybe you're a ghost!"

Another chill went up my spine.

"Joshua," Mrs. Finkel said, "didn't we just agree that you were going to do your best to behave in front of all your classmates—

including Stella?"

"Yeah," Joshua said.

"So, do you have anything to say?"

"I wasn't behaving badly," he said.

"Telling a classmate she may be a ghost does not count as good behavior," Mrs. Finkel said sternly.

"Fine," he said. "I'm sorry."

"Don't say it to me. Say it to Stella."

Joshua turned to me. "Sorry," he said.

"All right," Mrs. Finkel said. "You two should get back to your sleeping bags and start reading."

"What about my book?" I asked Mr. Ramos.

"I think you should give the new one a chance," Mr. Ramos said.

"The old one, you mean," Joshua said.

"Right."

"But I—" I started.

Mrs. Finkel picked up *My Missing Friend* and passed it to me. "Go on now, Stella," she said.

If I were Penny I would say, "That's not fair!" All the other kids got to check out the exact books they wanted. I was the only one who was given something different.

I walked back to my sleeping bag, where my friends were waiting for me. They were settling into their sleeping bags with their books—the ones they wanted to read.

"What happened?" Talisa asked. She had a smile on her face. She was almost laughing.

"What's so funny?" I asked her.

"I'm reading a joke book," she said. "And I read a really funny joke just now. Wanna hear it?"

We all said, "Okay."

"Okay, this isn't a knock-knock joke," Talisa said. "It's even better. Why is six afraid of seven?"

"Why?" we asked.

"Because seven ATE nine!" she said. "Get it—ate, instead of eight."

"That's funny," I told her.

"Then why aren't you laughing?"

"Because Mr. Ramos wouldn't let me trade my book. He said I had to keep this one."

"I thought we were allowed to read whatever we wanted," Talisa said.

"I thought so too," I said sadly.

"Poor Stella," Arielle said softly.

"Yeah, that's really bad luck," Lucy told me.

"I thought you didn't believe I would get bad luck," I said.

"I didn't say that exactly," Lucy said. "I

hope it's not catching."

"Here's another joke," Talisa said. "Knock knock."

"Who's there?" we asked.

"Boo."

"Boo who?"

"Don't cry, it's just me. The ghost!"

"Girls!" someone said, and we all screamed.

Mrs. Anderson came around the corner. "Mom, you scared us," Lucy said.

"I'm sorry," Mrs. Anderson said. "But you really do need to settle down now. You're making it hard for the other kids to read."

"Sorry," we all mumbled.

Mrs. Anderson walked away again, and my friends went back to their books—the books they'd picked out to read. I got into my sleeping bag. Even with my cozy socks on, I still felt a little chilly. Maybe because my shirt was still a bit damp. I burrowed in to try and get cozy, and slowly, slowly, slooooooooowly, I opened the book.

The first line said, "I used to have a friend named Catherine."

"Oooh," I said softly.

"What?" Lucy whispered.

"Nothing," I whispered back. "It's just scary already. She said she 'used to have a

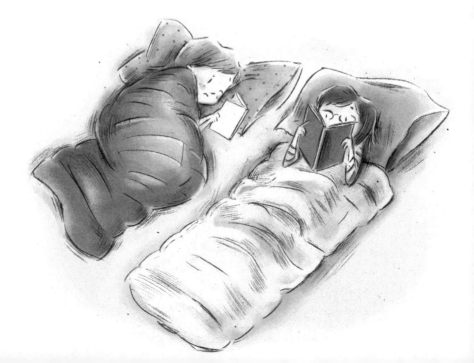

friend named Catherine,' which means she doesn't anymore. I think something awful happened to her."

"Maybe not," Lucy said. "Maybe she just moved away, like Willa did."

Willa used to be my best friend in Somers, before she moved to Pennsylvania. I guess it was possible that Catherine had moved away, too.

"You're right," I said. "She could've gone to Pennsylvania!"

"Or Transylvania," a voice said.

"What?"

"Transylvania," the voice said again. Lucy's lips weren't moving, so it wasn't her. Both Talisa and Arielle were reading, so I didn't think it was them either.

"Transylvaniiiiiiiia. Oooooooooooh." The voice sounded a little bit like a ghost but mostly like . . .

"JOSHUA!" Lucy said. She reached over me and poked through the little kids' books, to Joshua on the other side. "Stop listening to us and stop talking to us!"

"Lucy, stop yelling," Mrs. Anderson said.

Lucy stopped. Everyone was quiet again. The only sounds were soft leg kicks inside sleeping bags, and pages turning. I felt lonely, even though most of my friends were right there next to me. But they had their heads bent into their own books. It was like they were in their private book worlds. Usually my favorite part about reading is getting to be in a private book world. But I didn't want to go into the world of *My Missing Friend* all by myself. I didn't want to go into it at all.

Maybe Lucy was right. Maybe the other Stella B's friend just moved away, like my friend

Willa did. I only wanted to read the book if that was what happened, and I couldn't tell that on the first page. So I did something I'd never done before—I flipped to the last page of the book and read the very last line.

I'll miss you forever, my sweet friend Catherine.

That didn't sound like someone who had just moved away to me! What's the point of reading that book if it was going to have such a bad ending? I closed the book and burrowed deeper into my sleeping bag. I started to feel jealous of Evie, being home sick. I clicked my heels together three times, which is something I do sometimes when I have a wish to make. I got it from the movie *The Wizard of Oz*. And right then I really wanted to be home, just like Dorothy in the movie did! If I was home sick, I could read any of the books on my shelf that I wanted—and Mom would make me peppermint tea, too.

I closed the book and rested it on my chest. Mrs. Finkel walked by to check on us. She nodded toward my book, so I picked it up again. I turned to the first page and held it in front of my face so it would at least look like I was reading. But I wasn't going to actually read. That was my plan.

The problem is, when you stare at a page it's impossible NOT to read it. As soon as you know how to read, the words just automatically go into your brain. It's like breathing. You don't even think about it.

When Mum and Dad said we were moving to a castle, I didn't expect it to be so creaky and

old. I didn't expect there to be cobwebs in the
corners, and drafts under the doors. Mum said
it was the wind, but I knew it might be ghosts.

But then I met Catherine.

She told me to call her Cat. I'd never known
anyone with a name that was a word meaning
something else. But Cat wasn't like anyone I'd
ever met before. Her skin was white as bones.
Her hair was blue and green, like ocean waves.
Her eyes were yellow like the moonlight.

Yellow eyes! Those were the same eyes as
the ghost I'd seen when we were playing Ouija
board! I couldn't read anymore!

I closed the book again and tried to think
of happy things. Like dolphins, and the show
Superstar Sam, and getting to meet the star
whose real name is Thalia Lyn Blake, and eating fudge, and . . .

ARRRRGGGGHHHHH!!!!!!!!!!!!!!!!!!!!!!!!

No matter how hard I tried, I couldn't get
those scary book words out of my head. It was
like they were burned into my brain. I decided

I needed to read some other words—that was the only way to make those scary words disappear. I *needed* another book.

Even if I couldn't read *Tales of a Fourth Grade Nothing*, there were lots of books all around me. I was in a library after all!

Of course I needed a book that Mr. Ramos wouldn't see me taking, so that meant I had to pick a little kid book—because that was the section we'd set our sleeping bags up in. I looked at the shelf on my left and spotted *Days With Frog and Toad*.

I glanced around to make sure Mrs. Finkel and Mrs. Anderson weren't walking by to check on us. The coast was clear, so extra quickly, and EXTRA quietly, I pulled the book off the shelf.

"Hey," Lucy whispered. "What are you doing?"

I put a finger to my lips, which meant: Be quiet.

She watched as I opened up to the middle of *My Missing Friend*, and I slipped *Days With Frog and Toad* right there between the pages. And then I started reading again—but I was reading *Frog and Toad* instead. Just no one looking at me would be able to tell. In fact, Mrs. Finkel walked by right then, and she didn't suspect a thing! Lucy looked at me and winked. I winked back.

I finished the book in a few minutes, since it's only sixty-four pages and the type is pretty big. So then I flipped back to the first page and started reading again. Here's what Mr. Ramos didn't understand—sometimes it's nice to read something you've read already, even if it's a book for little kids, like for your younger sister. It's comfy like cozy socks, and

I stopped wishing I could go home.

I read the book two and a half times before Mrs. Finkel came by to announce it was time to put our books down and go to sleep. When she walked away, I slipped *Frog and Toad* back out, and put it on the shelf. Then I put *My Missing Friend* down. Right at the last minute, before Mr. Ramos turned the big lights off, I shoved it under my backpack so it'd be hidden away.

Then the lights went off. There was an eensy weensy bit of light coming in from the hallway outside the library doors, but that was it. It was mostly dark. I closed my eyes, and it got even darker. I planned to dream about all the not-scary things that Frog and Toad did together. And maybe I'd add my friends into the dream, and some dolphins, too.

CHAPTER 7

Yellow Eyes

I woke up because there was more bad luck: I had to go to the bathroom.

I hate having to go in the middle of the night, when you're cozy and warm in bed. (Or in this case, in my sleeping bag.) I kept my eyes closed and clicked my heels together three times, making a wish that the feeling would go away.

But of course it didn't work. I turned over and opened my eyes. And there, right in front of my face, were two eyes staring back at me. YELLOW eyes.

For a second my breath felt like it was caught in my throat. I closed my eyes again. It was late. Maybe my eyes were playing tricks on me, like Mrs. Anderson said.

But when I opened them, they were still there. My eyes hadn't been playing tricks on me before, and they weren't now.

"AHHHHHHHH!" I screamed.

The eyes blinked, and whoever it was—whatever it was—disappeared.

Around the room, I heard people's voices. Kids were saying, "Who screamed?" and "What happened?" and "Where am I again?" and "You're at school," and "Oh, yeah."

Flashlights clicked on. Lucy, Talisa, and Arielle gathered around me. "What's wrong?" they asked.

I heard footsteps walking toward us, and then a bang as whoever it was accidentally stubbed her toe on the corner of a bookshelf. "Ow," someone said.

"Mom, is that you?" Lucy asked.

"Yes," Mrs. Anderson said, stepping toward us. "It's me." In the dark, she looked strange and scary. Kind of like a ghost. "Is everyone all right?" she said, keeping her voice low.

"I saw those eyes again," I said.

Mrs. Anderson stepped over the other sleeping bags and crouched down next to me. "It's all right, Stella," she said. She petted my hair like I was a puppy. "It was just a bad dream."

"No, it wasn't!"

"Shh," she said.

"No, it wasn't," I said. "I woke up because

I had to go to the bathroom. I forgot to go before because I had to talk to Mr. Ramos about my book. And someone—or something—was staring at me."

Mrs. Finkel had appeared from around the corner, too. "Dreams can feel real when they're happening," she said.

"But I didn't see anything until I'd already opened my eyes," I said. "And there was a pair of yellow eyes staring back—no one in our class has yellow eyes. I don't think it was a person at all."

"Was it a ghost?" Arielle said, in a voice so soft it was like a breath.

"Probably," I said.

"Nonsense," Mrs. Finkel said. "Do you still need to go to the bathroom? Because I can take you now."

I still didn't want to get out of my sleeping

bag—more than ever I wanted to stay where it was cozy and warm. But when you gotta go, you gotta go. I picked up my flashlight and stood to follow Mrs. Finkel. But when I clicked the flashlight on, it didn't work. MORE bad luck.

At least my eyes had adjusted to the dark. I could see most things, or at least the shadows of most things. I was afraid to look around too much. What if I saw the eyes again?

"Careful not to step on anyone," Mrs. Finkel whispered as we walked through the main space of the library, where the boys were sleeping. Well, not all of them were sleeping. Joshua was awake and sitting up, and when I passed by him he said, "You had a bad dream, Smella?"

"Joshua," Mrs. Finkel hissed. I wondered if she'd send him home, even though it was

the middle of the night.

"Sorry, *Stella*," he said. "Did you have a bad dream?"

"No," I said.

"My cousin Bruce has bad dreams," he said. "But he's only five. He's practically a baby!"

"That's enough," Mrs. Finkel told him. "Come with me," she said to me. She walked faster, out of the library and into the hallway. I quickened my pace to catch up, and that's when I slipped and went smashing into the back of her, which was about the millionth bad-luck thing that had happened since the broken mirror.

"Oomph," Mrs. Finkel said.

"I'm sorry," I said. I thought she was about to be mad at me, because she'd been the one to say we shouldn't walk around in our socks. I could feel my cheeks heating up, and I knew they were turning pinker than cotton candy.

Then Mrs. Finkel did the most surprising thing ever. She reached out a hand for me to hold. "I'm sorry you're having a rough night," she said, and we walked the rest of the way to the bathroom like that.

A few minutes later I was done. I washed my hands and took off my socks to carry them back to the library—you can never be too careful about these things. When we turned the corner, I was expecting the library to look dark through the window. Instead it was all lit up.

Mrs. Finkel pushed open the door. Everyone was talking all at once.

Lucy rushed over to me. "You were right! There was something looking at you with yellow eyes! It was a cat!"

She pointed and I turned to see Mr. Haskell. He was holding a black cat in his arms—the bad-luck kind of cat!

Around me kids were asking all kinds of questions, and acting not afraid at all: "Can I pet it?" "Can I name it?" "I think Blackie would be a good name." "No, Blackie is a dumb name." "Don't say 'dumb,' Joshua."

That last one wasn't a kid talking—it was

Mrs. Finkel.

"What are we going to do with the cat now?" Talisa asked.

"Put it outside," Joshua said. "Duh."

"You can't put Blackie outside!" Asher said. "He'll get lost!"

"He's lost already."

"We're not putting this little guy—er, I mean girl—outside," Mr. Haskell said. "As long as no one's allergic, I think we'll let her stay for now, and deal with it tomorrow. Is anyone allergic?"

I thought about saying that I was allergic, but before I could, Mrs. Finkel answered for all the kids: "The only allergy in our class is a strawberry allergy," she said.

I wished Willa hadn't moved away to Pennsylvania, because she was allergic to cats (and just about everything else).

Mr. Haskell put the cat down and it started to walk around. Kids reached out to it, wanting it to sleep near them. But Mrs. Finkel told everyone to leave the cat alone and get back to their sleeping bags because she was about to turn off the lights again.

She counted to ten, and we all went back.

The room went dark, and I heard the sounds of people turning over in their sleeping bags, and their breaths getting deeper.

I didn't know how anyone could sleep with a cat prowling around the library. I clicked my heels together three times and wished to stay safe. And I kept my eyes open. In case my wish didn't work, I needed to remain on the lookout.

Even if that meant staying awake all night long. I squeezed the ball of cozy socks in my hand. I hadn't put them back on in case the cat came to attack me and I needed to get away fast. I didn't want to slip and fall again. Especially without Mrs. Finkel to catch me.

Someone moved, someone coughed, something creaked. There sure are a lot of sounds at night, and it's hard to tell which of them might be a cat. My heart pounded as hard as ever.

I don't know how much time passed. But it was A LOT of time. It felt like more time than had ever passed in a night before.

I was starting to feel sleepy. There'd been no sign of the cat. Maybe it had mysteriously disappeared from the library, just like it had mysteriously appeared. I let my eyes close, and I let my cheek sink a little deeper into the pillow under my head.

My backpack was behind me, and when I moved, it fell over onto my head. I opened my eyes and turned over to adjust it, and can you guess what I saw?

If you guessed THE CAT you are exactly right.

Its yellow eyes focused on me like lasers.

It jumped off my backpack and pawed at the floor underneath it. The cover of *My*

Missing Friend. I took my eyes off the cat just long enough to shake Lucy, who was sleeping closest to me. But all that happened was she muttered in her sleep and turned over onto her stomach.

I glanced back at the cat—it was batting at one of the straps on my backpack—and I climbed out to wake Talisa. But she was sleeping so soundly she didn't even mumble or move when I shook her.

I moved over to Arielle, but then I stopped myself. Arielle was more afraid of things than I was. It would be too mean to wake her up and get her scared about the cat.

I was awake by myself. I'd never felt so alone in my whole entire life; even more alone than it felt the last time, when everyone was reading right beside me. At least then they were awake, too.

With my heart still pounding, I turned back to look at the cat. It had managed to pull the book all the way out from under my bag. In the dark, by the glow of the cat's eyes, I could see the author's name—my name—on the cover.

I thought about Stella B's missing friend, Catherine. She called her Cat.

Suddenly I realized something. The scariest thing of all. And I swear my heart stopped in my chest for a few seconds.

Catherine. Cat. *Cat.*

"Psst. Here, kitty kitty kitty," someone whispered.

"Joshua? Is that you?" I whispered back.

"Stella?" He peeked his head around the corner. "Are you looking for the cat, too?"

I shook my head. "It's right here," I told him, pointing. It was nibbling the end of the

book. Or maybe it was trying to turn back the cover to read it.

Joshua tiptoed around the sleeping bags and plopped himself right on top of mine, so he could pet the cat. "I wouldn't do that if I were you," I told him.

"Why not?"

"Because I don't think it's a cat at all."

Joshua looked from me, to the cat, back to me again, and gave me a look like he thought I'd gone crazy. "It's got four legs, and a tail, and pointy ears, and it looks exactly like a cat," he said.

I nodded.

"So what on earth are you talking about?"

"You won't believe me if I tell you."

"Believe, believe, believe, you gotta believe," Lucy mumbled in her sleep; then she turned over.

Joshua scrunched up his face. "That was weird," he said, about Lucy. "Tell me anyway."

I stayed silent.

"Come on," he said, and his voice was almost above a whisper right then. I wished he would accidentally wake someone up. I knew he might get in trouble, but Joshua was always getting into trouble and he didn't seem to care. And then we wouldn't have to be alone.

But no one woke up. No one even stirred. Lucy didn't even mumble again.

"Tell me," Joshua said.

I took a deep, shaky breath. "Okay—I think the cat might be the ghost of the person from this book. Her name was Catherine—get it? Cat? Catherine? She disappeared a long time ago, and now the cat was trying to open the book like it wanted to read the story, or maybe it wanted to tell me something. You said there was a ghost who wanted to tell me something." I paused. Joshua didn't say anything. "You think that's crazy, don't you?"

"I have an idea," he said. He stood up to walk away. Part of me wanted to tell him not to go. I felt safer when he was with me. Isn't that crazy? I felt safer with JOSHUA!

"I'll be right back," he said. "And I'll bring the Ouija board."

CHAPTER 8

Cat Speaks

Joshua came back with the Ouija board and set it up at the bottom of my sleeping bag. "We don't need the triangle this time," he said. "We'll just ask the cat some questions. If she answers, we'll know it's the ghost." A chill raced through my body. Again. "Okay," I said.

"So make it stand up," he said.

"You do it."

"No, you."

"You're the one that said that's what we're

supposed to do."

"But you're the one it came over to sit with."

He had a point. "How about if we do rock-paper-scissors to decide," I said. So that's what we did.

"Rock, paper, scissors, shoot," we whispered together. I made my hand a fist, like a rock. But his hand was flat, like a piece of paper.

"Go on, Stella," he said.

"Two out of three?" I asked. But Joshua shook his head.

I moved the eensiest weensiest bit closer to the cat. "Here, kitty kitty," I said softly. I gave it the gentlest nudge from behind, and then I pulled my hand back right away, like I'd just touched a hot tray of fudge and burned myself.

Joshua and I watched as the cat stood up slowly and stretched its back. Then it plodded toward us. With each plod of its paws, my heart seemed to pound louder and louder. It stopped right in front of the board.

"Wow," Joshua said. "I think it really is the ghost with a message."

"So now what?"

"Now we have to ask what it wants to tell us."

We counted to three and whispered together: "What do you want to tell us."

The cat stood. Joshua's eyes were as big and round as gumballs. I couldn't see my own eyes, but I bet that's what they looked like, too.

The cat stepped on E, then N.

Joshua and I were whispering the letters out loud so we could remember them and figure out what they spelled.

It stepped on the T.

What was the word going to be? E-N-T-E-R? Enter where? Or maybe E-N-T-E-R-T-A-I-N, like it was going to put on a show for us. Or else maybe E-N-T-R-A-P. I'd learned that word when I'd made a fort of pillows for Baby Marco. Dad said I'd entrapped him, so he couldn't get out.

Oh no! Did the cat have a plan to entrap us?!

It lifted another paw. My breath was caught in my throat. Time seemed to be moving in slow motion as I waited to see where it would put its paw down.

It stepped on the 7.

As far as I knew there was no word in the whole entire world that started out as E-N-T-7.

The cat plopped itself down on the middle of the Ouija board and rested its head between its two front paws.

"Make it move again," Joshua told me.

I shook my head. "It's your turn," I said.

He whacked the board with the side of his palm. The cat lifted its head again, but it didn't move. "Come on," Joshua said, in a whisper-yell.

"SHHHHH," I told him. Then I whispered

to the cat, "Come on."

The cat didn't move. But someone else did. Mrs. Anderson.

I didn't even see her come up, but suddenly she was whisper-yelling herself: "Stella! Joshua! You're both supposed to be asleep right now."

"Stella woke me up," Joshua said.

"No, I didn't," I said. "You were looking for the cat and you came over here all by yourself."

"Oh yeah," he said. "I did. I couldn't sleep."

"I couldn't either," I said.

Mrs. Anderson nodded. "I'm sorry to hear that," she said. "But you shouldn't be playing a board game right now."

"But the cat came over," I started. "And . . . and . . ." How could I explain the next part?

"We thought it was a ghost from Stella's book and it was going to tell us a message,"

Joshua explained.

"I see," Mrs. Anderson said softly. Then she yawned and covered her mouth. "Excuse me."

"I'm sorry that we woke you up," I said. "It's just, well, I wanted to go to sleep but I couldn't. You can't make your body go to sleep when it doesn't want to."

"I understand," Mrs. Anderson said. "It can be a little bit scary to sleep away from home, huh?"

I nodded.

"Not me," Joshua said. "I'm not scared." But then the cat walked toward him and arched its back again, and Joshua gasped.

"I have an idea," Mrs. Anderson said. "If you two can do this very quietly—how about if you each grab your sleeping bag and pillow, and take them over to the corner over there where I'm sleeping? We can look out for each other, okay?"

Joshua and I both said, "Okay." He tiptoed back to the big room to get his sleeping bag and pillow, and I picked up mine as quietly as I could, and tiptoed to where Mrs. Anderson was waiting. I set myself up on her right side, and Joshua set up his sleeping bag and pillow on her left.

The cat followed us over and sat right at our feet. It laid its head on the end of my sleeping bag, and its body was stretched out so that the tip of its tail was on Joshua's. Maybe the cat was lonely, like I'd been. Maybe it was looking for company so it wouldn't have to feel so alone.

I was still scared, but not as scared as I had been before, because Mrs. Anderson was right there. She said she'd wait to go to sleep

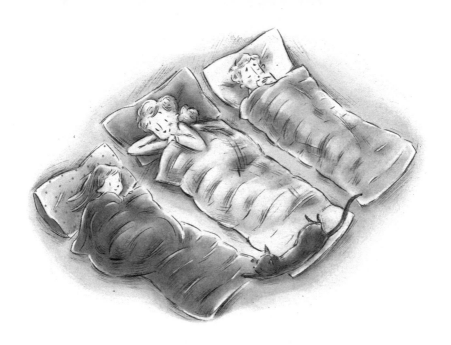

until we did. I closed my eyes. Then I opened them just slightly and looked across Mrs. Anderson to see if Joshua had closed his, too. He had. So I closed mine again.

I thought I'd stay awake forever, but I must have fallen asleep. Because I didn't wake up until someone was above me shouting, "Hey! Stella! What are you doing all the way over here?"

I opened my eyes, and there was Lucy. Talisa and Arielle were with her, too.

Next to me, Mrs. Anderson's sleeping bag was smoothed out and empty. And on the other side was Joshua's crumpled sleeping bag. He was gone, and so was the cat.

It was so weird. It was like a dream that hadn't really happened. But when I got up and walked back with my friends, I saw the Ouija board and box in the little kids' reading nook, and the book that started it all was on the floor right next to it.

So I knew it had all happened in real life after all.

Pretty soon everyone was awake. Lucy said she didn't know where the cat was, and neither did Talisa or Arielle. But it didn't matter. The sun was streaming through the windows. Everyone was awake. I didn't feel lonely anymore. In fact, if I saw the cat I might even bend down to pet it.

Maybe.

But there were other things to do. The grown-ups said to brush our teeth, roll up our sleeping bags, and make everything in the library look clean and neat, like we'd never been there. Joshua put the Ouija board back where it belonged. The cat was nowhere to be seen, but I found out that was because Asher's dad had taken it home early in the morning.

"How come Asher gets the cat?" Joshua asked.

"He doesn't get to keep it," Mr. Ramos said. "It's not his cat. But the Haskells have other cats at home, so Asher's family has everything on hand that it needs for now— food, toys, a litter box."

A litter box—ew, gross.

"And," Mr. Ramos went on, "we can all put our heads together to figure out how to get the cat back to its real family as quickly as possible."

"Once Stella lost Evie's dog and we made posters," Lucy said. I knew she was trying to be helpful, but I hated remembering that. It was one of the worst times of my whole entire life. Bella, Evie's puppy, was missing for two days! I'd worried we'd never find her!

"Do you have paper?" Lucy asked Mr. Ramos. "I can make signs up for the cat."

"They have to be opposite of your other signs," Talisa broke in. "These will say 'Found Cat' instead of 'Lost Dog.'"

"Right," Lucy said. "Do you have a cell phone, Mr. Ramos? Can you text Mr. Haskell to take a picture of the cat before he comes back here? We can print it out and put it on the signs. He's coming back, right?"

"Yes, he is," Mr. Ramos said. "He has to pick Asher up. But I do think we're getting a little ahead of ourselves."

"No, we're not," Lucy said.

"What's going on here?" Mrs. Anderson asked. She'd come up behind Lucy and put her hands on her shoulders.

"We were talking about the cat," Lucy explained.

"Of course, the cat," Mrs. Anderson said. "*Just* a cat," she added, and she winked at me.

Mrs. Finkel clapped her hands and we all had to quiet down.

"Kids, please pick up all your belongings," Mrs. Finkel said. "We'll walk together, in an ORDERLY fashion, to have breakfast. Your parents will be picking you up from there."

CHAPTER 9

Good Luck

Guess who was in the lunchroom when we got there?

If you said Evie, then you are exactly right!

She was sitting at our table, which already had plates and forks and knives and napkins set up. She was wearing the exact same out-fit I was—without a juice stain on her shirt. And there was something on her chin, but I couldn't tell what it was from far away.

I started to run to her, but Mrs. Finkel said, "Stella, no running! And please put your belongings over by the far window before you take your seat."

So I walked, as quickly as I could, to drop my sleeping bag and backpack by the window, and then I walked even faster back to the table, and sat down next to Evie. "Oh my goodness!" I said. "There's a bandage on your chin! What happened?"

"Just some bad luck," she said. "I tripped when I was walking Bella and landed on my chin. I needed seven stitches."

"Wow," I said. "I'm sorry."

"You don't have to be sorry," she said. "It wasn't your fault."

"I think it might've been," I admitted. "I broke a mirror yesterday, and all these bad-luck things started happening. First I found a book about a real-live ghost, and then Mr. Moyers yelled at dinner."

Arielle glanced around. "I don't see him now," she said softly. She'd sat down across from us. Talisa sat next to her, and Lucy sat on my other side.

"Maybe he decided not to come back today," Talisa said.

"I hope so," Lucy and I said at the same time.

"Jinx!" Talisa said.

Then we had to say each other's names backwards. "I didn't even tell you about the cat yet," I told Evie.

"A cat?"

"Yup," I said. And I would have told her more, but then Lucy called out. "Joshua, you're too mean to Stella. You can't sit with us."

It was nice that Lucy stood up for me, but

I felt bad for Joshua. "I don't mind if Joshua sits with us," I said. "He is my friend."

"Really?" Lucy asked.

I nodded. "Today he is."

"Knock knock," Talisa said.

"Who's there?"

"It's Opposite Day!"

"You mean it's *not* Opposite Day," Lucy said. "That's what you say on Opposite Day, because it's really the opposite."

"It's not Opposite Day," I said. "And I mean it's really not. Joshua can stay. Okay?"

The other girls nodded. Then Lucy got down to business. "We need to talk about our signs," she said.

"Signs?" Evie asked.

"It has to do with the cat I mentioned before. You see—"

"Stella! STEL-LAAAAAAH!" a voice

rang out.

I turned to see Penny racing toward us. "Don't run," I told her, before she could get in trouble with Mrs. Finkel. I didn't know for sure if a third-grade teacher could get mad at a kindergartener, but it was better not to take the chance.

Penny stopped running and she speed-walked the rest of the way to our table. When she got to us she was huffing and puffing a little. Lucy scooted over so Penny could sit between us, next to me.

"What are you doing here?" I asked.

"I'm not supposed to tell you because Mom and Dad are helping to make a special breakfast," she told me.

Talisa clapped her hands. "Ooh, your parents are making a special breakfast? Does that mean we'll be eating candy?"

"Oops," Penny said.

"Don't worry," I said. "We won't tell them you told us anything."

Everyone pinky-swore to make it official.

Penny started giggling. "What's so funny?" Lucy asked.

"We're having breakfast in the *lunchroom*!" she said. "It's so funny!"

It *was* funny. The rest of us laughed, too.

"I always wanted to see Somers Elementary School on a weekend," Penny went on. "And now I have!"

"Do you know what you want to see next?" Arielle asked.

"Hmm," Penny said, thinking. "Oh, I know! I want to see the White House!"

The rest of us at the table agreed that the White House would be a pretty cool thing to see.

Then we started talking about the cat signs again. It was actually good that Penny was there, because she was the one who put the signs up in the exact place where Bella the dog had run away to, and we ended up finding Bella because of it.

Penny had lots of ideas about where we

could put the "Found Cat" signs. Like she said we should definitely put signs up by Man's Best Friend, which is the pet store in the same shopping center as Batts Confections. "Because if someone lost their cat they might go try to get a new one," she said.

We were so busy making plans for who would put signs up on what streets, that we didn't notice who had walked up behind us: MR. MOYERS!

"Children," he said, in his deep crackly voice. If it was possible, Mr. Moyers looked even older and meaner than usual. The bags under his eyes were bigger, his eyes were smaller, and the few strands of hair on his mostly bald head were sticking up, like he hadn't brushed them down after he'd woken up. "Did I hear you talking about a cat in school?"

Penny pressed herself closer to me and I

put an arm around her.

"We didn't break any rules," Lucy said quickly. "We didn't bring a cat to school. We found one."

"Where?" he asked gruffly.

I could feel Penny's body shaking against me. Sometimes protecting my little sister makes me feel braver. "It came into the library when we were supposed to be sleeping," I said.

"What color was it?"

"Black."

"That's what I thought," Mr. Moyers said. "Is it in the library now?"

"Asher's dad took it home," Talisa supplied.

"Why'd he do that?"

"They have other cats at home. It needed food, and a place to go to the bathroom."

Mr. Moyers folded his arms across his

chest and stared down at us with his beady eyes.

"You can ask my mom about the cat if you don't believe us," Lucy said.

Mr. Moyers blinked and grunted. Then he left to walk over to Lucy's mom.

"Now back to the signs," Lucy said.

But we didn't get to talk about the signs anymore, because then breakfast was served. And you'll never guess what it was, so I'll just tell you:

Pancakes.

Okay, maybe you would've guessed pancakes. But you'd really never guess what was mixed up in them:

Eensy weensy pieces of my STELLA'S FUDGE!

Mom and Dad came out from the kitchen and helped the other grown-ups serve all us kids. "Is Marco here?" Lucy asked. "I want to hold him."

"Marco is with his babysitter, Mrs. Miller," Mom said. "And you have to eat your pancakes anyway."

We ate our first pancakes so fast and asked for seconds. "Hey, Stella, knock knock," Talisa said.

"Who's there?" I asked.

"Pancake."

"Pancake who?"

"The best pancakes in the whole world!"

I speared a fluffy piece of pancake with a chunk of chocolate swirl fudge and popped it in my mouth. And as I chewed I nodded in agreement. They were the best pancakes I've ever had in my whole entire life!

Mrs. Finkel stood in front of the tables and clapped her hands so we'd all quiet down. She said she had a few announcements to make. "First, when you finish eating I want you to clean up in an ORDERLY fashion. For those of you whose parents aren't already here, your parents should be arriving in the next ten minutes. Second, I am sure you'll all be interested to know the cat's owner has been found."

Kids started clapping before Mrs. Finkel had stopped talking, so it was hard to hear what she was saying.

"Shh, shh," I said.

"Mr. Moyers has a story to tell you," Mrs. Finkel said.

Mr. Moyers looked pinched and uncomfortable, but we stayed quiet and he started talking. "Right after my wife died, I adopted a cat."

I'd never even thought about Mr. Moyers having a wife. Suddenly, for the first time ever, I felt sorry for Mr. Moyers.

"It was a black cat," he said. "Because they were always my wife's favorite. She knew some folks were afraid of them. But she always said they needed a good home as much as any other cat did."

"It was YOUR cat we found!" Lucy said.

"I believe it was," Mr. Moyers said. "When I left the house to come here last night, she snuck out after me. She's very attached to me. I always have to be careful when I leave that she doesn't follow me out. Apparently I wasn't careful enough last night. When I got home, she was gone. I drove around looking for her all night."

"I'll tell my mom to bring her back to

you!" Asher called out.

"Lucy's mom already made that call," Mrs. Finkel said.

Mr. Moyers smiled. "Thank you," he said.

"Wow," I said softly.

"What?" Mom asked me.

"That was the first time I've ever seen Mr. Moyers smile in my whole entire life."

"Maybe he's lonely," Mom said. "Maybe that cat is his companion."

"What's the cat's name?" Penny asked.

I shrugged. "I don't know," I told her.

"Hey, Mr. Moyers!" Lucy called out.

I thought he'd tell her not to shout. But he walked over to us and said, "Yes?"

"Does the cat have a name?"

"Catherine," he said.

I felt a chill run up my spine—again!

"It was my wife's name," Mr. Moyers added. "When she died, I missed her very much. I even missed calling her name. So I named the cat after her. It was my good luck that she wandered in here and you found her."

Good luck! That was a first!

"And it's good luck that you work here," Lucy added. "And that you heard us talking about her."

"I work here because my wife did," Mr. Moyers said. "It's how we met—many, many years before any of you were born. Being here reminds me of her."

"Cool," Eleanor said from the table next to ours.

"Can we visit the cat named Catherine?" Beatrice asked.

Mr. Moyers shook his head. "You kids should concentrate on your studies," he said. "That's the problem with kids these days. They're too distracted." He cleared his throat and walked away from our table, stopping to bend and pick up a napkin that Miles had accidentally dropped on the floor. "You kids need to clean up after yourselves!"

So he was back to being the regular scary old Mr. Moyers again. Except he wasn't as scary as he used to be.

"It's so weird his wife was named Catherine," I said. "Like Catherine in the library book. Maybe when she died she became a ghost!"

"What book is that?" Mom asked.

"Oh, this book called *My Missing Friend*."

"By someone named Stella B?" Mom asked.

"Yeah, how'd you know?"

"Because that was one of my favorite books when I was young," Mom said. "It's where I first heard the name Stella, and I always wanted to get you a copy but it's out of print. I'm so happy you'll get to read it!"

"But I don't want to read it," I told her. "Because of the missing friend—it's too scary to read about Catherine who died."

"Stella," Mom said. "You know I don't believe in giving away the endings to books, but I'm going to make an exception here. Catherine didn't die. She wasn't alive in the first place."

"I don't understand."

"She was Stella's imaginary friend, and she went missing when Stella grew up. I think the other Stella B was a lot like you—she had an active imagination, and she loved writing."

"But her name was Catherine, and Mr. Moyers's wife was named Catherine," I said.

"Quite a coincidence, isn't it?" Mom said. "But that's all it is, still, I promise."

I stood up. "I'll be right back," I said.

"Where are you going?"

"I have to tell Mr. Ramos that I actually want to check out that book!"

Pretty soon after that it was time to go. Dad, Mom, Penny, and I got into the car together. "Good-bye, school!" Penny called out the window. "See you on Monday!"

"Yeah, see you," I said.

I liked Somers Elementary School on the weekend. But I like being with my family on the weekend, too. In fact I think being home in my room with my parents nearby is the perfect place to read a book.

When I got home that's just what I did.

Courtney Sheinmel

Courtney Sheinmel is the author of over a dozen books for kids and teens, including *Zacktastic*, *Sincerely*, and *Edgewater*. Like Stella Batts, she was born in California and has a younger sister, but unlike Stella, her parents never owned a candy store. Courtney lives in New York City, and hopes you'll visit her online at www. courtneysheinmel.com.

Jennifer A. Bell

Jennifer A. Bell is an illustrator whose work can be found on greeting cards, in magazines, and in more than two dozen children's books. After several years of living in Minneapolis, Minnesota, she recently relocated to Toronto, where she lives with her husband, son, and cranky cat. Visit her online at www.JenniferABell.com.

Praise for Stella Batts

Other books in this series:

Meet Stella and friends online
at www.stellabatts.com

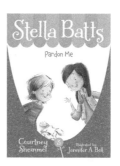

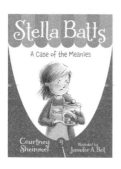